Magicat

JENNIFER
GRAY

AMANDA
SWIFT

Illustrated by
Richard Watson

For Barnabé – J.G.

For Lisa – A.S.

First published in 2020 in Great Britain by
Barrington Stoke Ltd
18 Walker Street, Edinburgh, EH3 7LP

www.barringtonstoke.co.uk

Text © 2020 Jennifer Gray & Amanda Swift
Illustrations © 2020 Richard Watson

A CIP catalogue record for this book is available
from the British Library upon request

ISBN: 978-1-78112-925-8

Printed in China by Leo

Contents

CHAPTER 1

Magicat Arrives

"It's really dark and misty!" Jessie said as she stood on her doorstep and looked up at the night sky. "It's perfect for Halloween. We might even meet a real witch!"

Jessie loved everything to do with magic, especially stories about witches and wizards. Halloween was her favourite night of the year and most of all she liked trick or treating.

"Hurry up, Ali!" Jessie said.

Ali was Jessie's best friend. He and Jessie were in the same class at school. Ali's house was at the back of Jessie's, so their gardens were joined.

"Wait!" Ali called out to Jessie. "My beard is falling off. I want to be the best wizard on the street!"

Jessie waited while Ali fixed his false beard back on and then they set off together.

They ran down the street with their treat buckets swinging in their hands. Jessie's mum was just behind them. Lots of the houses had pumpkins in the windows and fake spiderwebs round the doors. There were groups of children going up and down the road in all kinds of spooky outfits. *If one of them really is a witch*, thought Jessie, *no one would know*. It was almost pitch-black, apart from the street lights and the moon and stars.

"Hang on a minute," said Jessie, "now my false fingernail's fallen off." Jessie had green fingernails to match the green make-up on her face.

"You'll just have to be a witch who bites her nails," Ali said.

They both giggled.

Jessie walked up to the first door. "Have you got a trick?" she whispered. "Just in case?" Ali loved tricks as much as Jessie loved magic.

"I've got three! Hope we get the chance to use them all!" Ali patted his pocket.

Jessie knocked on the door. A woman opened it. "Trick or treat?" Jessie said.

"Here's a treat!" said the woman. She gave Jessie and Ali some sweets.

They ate one or two each but left the rest until they got home.

"I love sweets but I hope someone asks for a trick!" Ali said.

Up and down the street they went. They took turns to knock on the doors. Jessie's mum met a friend and they started to chat together. Jessie and Ali had great fun shouting "Trick or treat!" but everyone gave them treats rather than asking for a trick.

Ali and Jessie turned the corner of the street. "Oh no," said Jessie. "It's Eddie Biggs and his gang. They always spoil everything.

Look! They haven't even dressed up for Halloween."

Eddie Biggs went to their school. So did his friends. Eddie was a bully. He enjoyed making fun of other children and scaring them as much as he could. He had very short hair and a mean look on his face. He wore big black boots and walked along with his hands in his pockets, chewing gum. So did his friends.

And the worst thing about Eddie Biggs was that he lived next door to Jessie.

"I know who you are," said Eddie.

"No, you don't," said Jessie. "I'm a witch and he's a wizard, and we're just here for Halloween."

"There's no such thing as witches and wizards," said Eddie.

"How do you know?" Jessie said bravely.

"It's obvious. You're Jessie and you're Ali. You've just got black bin bags as capes and black wellies. You're not a real witch and wizard. I saw you make your hats at school. They're rubbish."

Eddie knocked Ali's hat off his head. Ali bent to pick it up.

"Stop it, you bully!" Jessie yelled.

6

Eddie reached out and grabbed Jessie's treat bucket. Then he turned and ran off down the road. His gang ran off too.

"He's taken my sweets!" said Jessie.

"I wish I'd done one of my tricks on him ..." Ali said.

Jessie sighed. She wished she could do a *real* magic spell on Eddie.

Just then there was a loud whoosh! Suddenly the sky was lit up by a shower of gold light. The children looked up.

"Wow!" said Ali. "That's the first firework I've seen this year. It's fantastic! I hope there are more ..."

"I don't," said Jessie. "Not if it's the same people letting them off. Look."

Ali looked down the road to where Jessie was pointing. Eddie's big brother was showing off to Eddie and his gang by lighting another firework.

Jessie looked around to check if Mum was nearby but she couldn't see her. She must still be round the corner, chatting to her friend.

Another firework whooshed into the air. As Jessie and Ali watched the green stars fall through the dark, they saw two sparks that seemed brighter and bigger than the rest. And they seemed to be coming very fast towards *them*!

As the sparks got nearer, Jessie and Ali saw that they weren't sparks at all. They were eyes. They were green eyes. Green eyes on a black and white body. And they were getting nearer and nearer until suddenly ...

PLONK!

Something landed in Ali's treat bucket.

"It's a cat!" Jessie gasped.

The cat was very small. It curled its tail neatly round its body and it held a tiny book. It looked up at them with its head on one side and its green eyes wide open.

"Trick or treat?" asked the cat.

Jessie and Ali stared back at it. They were so shocked they didn't know what to say!

How come you can talk? thought Ali.

I wish I had a cat like that, thought Jessie.

"Trick or treat?" the cat said again.

"I don't want a trick," said Ali at last. "I've got my own."

"Good, because I'm the treat," said the cat. "I'm Magicat."

CHAPTER 2

Magicat Needs a Home

"Magicat?" Jessie asked. "Do you mean you're *really* magic?"

"Of course I am," said Magicat.

"Wow!" said Ali. "How did you get here?"

"I fell off a broomstick." Magicat looked cross. "*Someone* let off a firework while I was reading my book of spells ..."

"That was Eddie Biggs and his brother," Jessie told him quickly, in case Magicat thought it was them. "They're both horrible."

"Humph," said Magicat. "Someone should teach them some manners."

"What were you doing on the broomstick?" Ali asked.

"Flying of course!" Magicat said.

"Yes, but who with?" Jessie said.

"My witch!" Magicat said, and looked sadly at the sky. "Her name is Wenna. And I don't think it's safe for her to come and fetch me tonight, thanks to those nasty boys."

"Well, why don't you stay for a sleepover with Jessie and me, and she can come and fetch you tomorrow?" said Ali.

Magicat shook his head. "She's only supposed to fly on Halloween."

"But why?" Ali asked.

"Because on Halloween, *real* witches and wizards can fly and no one bothers about them," Jessie said. "The rest of the time they stay at home."

"Exactly," Magicat said. "You see, humans used to pick on witches in the old days. That's why the witches had to move to Magic Land to get away."

"Is that where you live?" Jessie asked.

"Yes," Magicat replied. "Crab Cave, Witch Island, Magic Land." He put his head on one side and looked Jessie up and down. "But I'd be very happy to stay with you until my witch finds a way to come and get me. It'll be like a holiday."

Jessie had never felt so excited in her life. She had always wanted a cat, and a magic one was even better. It was a dream come true.

Just then Eddie Biggs walked up to them again. He was kicking a tin can.

Jessie's heart sank. "Quick, hide!" she ordered. "It's Eddie. If he finds out you come from Magic Land, he'll take you from us."

She pushed Magicat down into Ali's treat bucket. Ali quickly covered Magicat up with his false beard.

Eddie Biggs stopped. "Who were you talking to?" he asked.

"No one," Jessie said.

"A-shoo!" The sound of a sneeze came from the bucket.

"What was that?" Eddie wanted to know.

"It was me," said Ali. "I've got a cold."

"You didn't have one ten minutes ago," Eddie said.

"A-shoo!" the noise came again.

"I get them very quickly," said Ali. He winked at Jessie, then slid his hand into his pocket.

Jessie tried hard not to laugh. Ali was going to play one of his tricks!

"Oh no, I think I'm going to sneeze again!" Ali pulled his hand out of his pocket and cupped his hands over his nose. "AA-AA-SHOO!" he cried.

"See?" said Jessie as Ali took his hands down from his face. "He told you he had a cold."

Ali's face and hands were covered in yellow gunk.

"Yuk! That's horrible!" Eddie Biggs backed away.

"You'd better not come any closer then," Jessie warned.

"Don't worry, I won't!" Eddie shouted as he ran off down the street.

"That was brilliant!" Jessie said, and handed Ali some tissues. "Where did you get that stuff?"

Ali wiped his face. "I found it in the junk yard in an old trunk," he said. "I think it was from an old Halloween fancy-dress kit."

The junk yard was in Ali's garden. Ali's dad never threw anything away and Ali was always finding interesting things that he could use for pranks.

"A-shoo!" This time the false beard flew up and over the side of Ali's bucket. Magicat's head popped up. He looked very cross and he was still sneezing and spluttering. "I could have done some real magic on that horrible boy!" he moaned. "You should have let me."

"You can't," Jessie told him. "At least not in public. You just told us that. You might get picked on like the witches and wizards did, remember?"

"Especially by Eddie," Ali said.

Magicat looked cross. "What can I do then?"

"Act like a normal cat," Ali said. "Just sit about and purr. Maybe chase mice if you see any."

"That sounds boring," said Magicat. "I'd much rather do some magic." He yawned. "Can we go home now?"

"First, you have to promise to pretend to be a normal cat," Jessie said.

"Oh, all right!" moaned Magicat. "Is it OK if I snore?"

Jessie and Ali laughed.

"Yes," said Jessie. "Normal cats snore."

"Good," said Magicat.

He shut his eyes and fell asleep. He began to snore softly.

"Look! Your mum's coming," said Ali to Jessie. "What are we going to tell her?"

Jessie's mum was walking towards them.

"Let's just say we found him in the street," Jessie said.

"You're not going to tell *her* he's magic, are you?" Ali asked.

"Of course not!" Jessie grinned. "That's our secret."

CHAPTER 3
Magicat's Sleepover

"What is this soft fluffy thing?" asked Magicat.

"A cushion," answered Ali.

"It's SO lovely, SO soft and SO fluffy, it's like sitting on a cloud," purred Magicat as he curled up on the cushion.

"Have you ever sat on a cloud?" asked Jessie.

"Of course not, you'd fall right through it!" Magicat told her.

Jessie, Ali and Magicat were all up in Jessie's bedroom. Jessie was tucked up in her

bed and Ali was lying on a mattress next to her with Magicat at the bottom.

"I'm so glad Mum and Dad let you stay," said Jessie. "I've always wanted a cat."

"I can see that," said Magicat. All over the walls there were pictures of cats, and Jessie's pyjamas had cat prints on. Then he looked at Ali. "And would you like a pet dinosaur?" he asked. Ali's pyjamas had dinosaurs on them.

Ali laughed. "No, I don't think a dinosaur would make a very good pet," he said.

"You're right," said Magicat. "Even if they didn't want to eat you, they'd need an enormous cushion as their bed."

"And think of the food!" said Jessie.

"You'd need a whole trolley full just for the dinosaur," said Ali.

"Do the pets in your land get fed even if they don't do any work?" asked Magicat.

"Yes," said Ali. "Don't they in Magic Land?"

"No," said Magicat. "In Magic Land we have to learn the spells, catch what we need to make them, carry it all back to the cave, help with spell-making *and* balance on the broomstick. And we don't have any cushions."

"Really?" asked Jessie.

"Yes, really. All the cats sleep on the ground. Sometimes we use each other as pillows."

"Maybe you should just stay here for ever," said Ali.

Magicat suddenly jumped up.

"No thanks," he said. "I still have so much to learn. And I don't want to get behind the other cats in my magic class. If it takes Wenna too long to fetch me, they'll have finished *A Cat's Book of Magic: Book Two* and I'll still be on *Book One*." He started to sob loudly.

"You could write Wenna a letter and tell her where you are. That will help her find you," Jessie said.

Magicat sat up straight. He stopped sobbing.

"Great idea," said Magicat. "Where's the paper?"

Jessie got out a pad of paper and a pencil from the desk next to her bed. Magicat sat on the pillow next to her.

"What's that?" he asked.

"It's a pencil," said Ali. "You write with it."

"Oh," said Magicat. "In Magic Land we write with a feather pen, but I'll have a go with this stick."

He picked up the pencil in his paws and started to write ...

When he had finished, Magicat put the pencil down. "I've told her where I am and asked her to come and get me," he said.

"Good," said Jessie.

"Yes, it is good. It's a very good letter," said Magicat. "Have you got an envelope?"

"Here we are," said Jessie, getting an envelope out of her desk.

Magicat wrote in big letters:

WENNA WITCH
CRAB CAVE
WITCH ISLAND
MAGIC LAND

"Do you need a stamp on your envelope?" said Ali.

"What, and spoil my lovely letter with your big feet? No thanks!" said Magicat.

"But how will the letter get there?" said Jessie.

"Like this of course." Magicat got up from the pillow. He pointed his tail at the letter and said:

Fly away over land and wave,
Straight to Wenna Witch's cave!

All of a sudden his fur stood up on end. His green eyes shone bright. Sparks flew from his tail.

FLASH!

BANG!

The window shot open.

Jessie and Ali laughed and clapped as the letter flew into the air and out into the night.

CHAPTER 4

Magicat Makes Breakfast

The next morning when Jessie woke up, Magicat wasn't there.

"Quick!" She shook Ali awake. "We'd better make sure he's not getting into any trouble."

The two children raced downstairs.

Magicat was by himself in the kitchen reading his book of spells. "Did you see Mum and Dad this morning?" Jessie asked.

"Yes. Your mum's gone to the office and your dad's gone to the bathroom. Is he a plumber?" Magicat said.

"No, he fixes computers," said Jessie. "He must have gone to the bathroom before he started work in his study."

"Oh, I see," said Magicat. "I suppose I do the same in Magic Land. Although we don't have a bathroom. I poo in the woods and then do my spells in the cave."

"Did you remember to behave like a normal cat in front of my mum and dad?" Jessie asked.

"Of course I did!" Magicat said. "I purred and everything. But I couldn't find any mice to chase: only an old peanut."

"That was a cool trick you did with the letter last night," said Ali. "Can you do another one?"

"Of course I can," Magicat said. "How about I magic you some breakfast?"

"That's a good idea," said Jessie. "I'm starving."

"What would you like?" said Magicat.

"Pancakes," Ali said, "with honey and ice cream."

"Are you sure you don't want a bowl of bugs?" said Magicat.

Jessie shook her head. "Yuk! No, thanks."

Magicat sighed. "All right, but you'll have to get things out of the cupboards for me. I can't open them with my paws."

The children got everything ready with Magicat watching:

Flour
Eggs
Milk
Honey
Ice cream.

"Do you need a bowl to make the pancake mix?" asked Jessie.

Magicat looked surprised. "Don't you have a cauldron?"

Jessie shook her head. "No. Sorry." She got out a large mixing bowl.

"What about a fire?" Magicat asked.

"Just the cooker, I'm afraid." Jessie found a frying pan and placed it on the hob. She looked over at Ali and winked. At this rate it would be quicker to make the pancakes themselves!

"Stand back while I make the mixture," Magicat ordered.

The children stepped away.

Magicat pointed his tail at the bowl:

Box of eggs and bag of flour,
You must obey my special power,
In the bowl now quickly mix,
And some pancakes I will fix.

Magicat's fur stood up on end. His green eyes
shone bright. Sparks flew from his tail. A cloud
of flour puffed out of the bag into the bowl,
followed by the eggs, which cracked themselves.
The children watched as the eggshells threw
themselves into the bin, the jug tipped
some milk over the top of the bowl, and the
ingredients mixed themselves together.

Magicat opened one eye. "Did it work?"

"Yes!" said Jessie. "Why wouldn't it?"

"No reason," said Magicat.

"Do the next bit," Ali begged.

"Don't rush me!" Magicat grumbled. "It's not that easy, you know!" He pointed his tail at the pan:

In the pan and on the fire,
Toss them higher and higher and higher,
A dab of honey, then add ice cream,
To conjure up a breakfast dream!

The jug dipped into the pancake mix and poured some into the pan. The pan began to sizzle. Then it flipped the pancake up into the air.

"Awesome!" Ali said.

"I told you I could do it," Magicat said proudly.

But instead of dropping into the pan, the pancake landed with a SPLAT on the floor. Then great dollops of honey began to fly out of the jar and onto the pancake on the floor; great dollops of ice cream bombed after it like snowballs. Meanwhile the jug was hard at work pouring more mixture into the pan. Everything was happening at once.

Soon the kitchen was a total mess. There were pancakes on the floor, pancakes on the ceiling and pancakes on the bench. Everything was covered in sticky honey and ice cream.

The children looked on – this was awful! "Can't you make it stop?" Jessie cried.

"Not exactly," said Magicat as a scoop of ice cream hit him on the head.

"What do you mean, 'not exactly'?" Ali gasped as a splodge of honey hit him in the eye.

"I haven't learned how to stop spells yet!"

"You could have told us!" said Jessie.

"You didn't ask!" Magicat grabbed his spell book and hid under the table away from the flying food.

Jessie and Ali joined him.

"Now what?" said Ali.

"I don't know!" said Magicat crossly. "It's not my fault. Anyway, how can I work with no cauldron and no fire? Plus, I normally perform spells in a *cave*! It's just not *witchy* enough here—"

SPLAT! The final pancake landed on the floor in a soggy heap beside his tail. There was silence in the kitchen.

Just then the kitchen door opened. It was Dad. "What on earth?" he said.

"Oh no!" whispered Ali. "Now we're in trouble."

CHAPTER 5

Magicat Makes a Cat Cave

By the time Jessie and Ali had cleared up the mess and had breakfast it was nearly time for lunch!

"I could magic you some lunch," Magicat said.

"NO!" cried Jessie and Ali together. If the magic went wrong again, they didn't want to do any more clearing up.

"Or a drink? I can do a very nice frog and onion smoothie."

"I'm not thirsty," said Ali. Actually, he *was* thirsty but he didn't want to tell Magicat that frog and onion smoothie sounded disgusting.

Magicat sulked. He curled up on the floor and tucked his head under his tail.

"OK," he said. "I'll just go to sleep for a day or two. You can make your own meals."

Jessie had an idea. "Maybe you DO need a cave to do your spells," she said.

Magicat lifted his head. "Are there any caves round here?" he asked.

"No," said Jessie. "But I know somewhere we could turn into a pretend cave. Come with me."

Jessie led the way into the garden. She crossed the lawn to the shed. "What about this?" she said, and opened the door.

Magicat poked his head in. "I like the cobwebs and the beetles but it's still not witchy enough," he huffed.

"I know what to do," said Ali. "Follow me."

Ali led the way to the bottom of the garden where there was a fence. On the other side of the fence there was loads and loads of junk.

"That's *my* garden," said Ali proudly.

"Really?" said Magicat. "It doesn't look like a garden. It looks like a junk yard."

"Well, it's a junk yard *and* a garden," Ali explained. "My dad loves junk. And I love turning junk into pranks."

'What's a prank?" asked Magicat.

"It's a way of tricking people without magic," said Ali. "Like the snot trick I did on Eddie Biggs."

"Let's see if we can find some witchy stuff," said Jessie as she squeezed through a little gap in the fence. Ali and Magicat squeezed through after her. They made their way through the junk and found some broomsticks, a big iron pot that looked like a cauldron and a couple of stools. They carried them back to the shed.

"Much better!" said Magicat when they had finished. "It looks very witchy – just like my cave in Magic Land. Would you like me to try a spell now?"

"Yes, please," said Jessie. "What can you do?"

"I can do a spell to make your nose longer," Magicat said. "The witches are very keen on that one. They do it on each other as a birthday present."

"I like my nose as it is," said Jessie.

"What about an enormous wart?" Magicat asked.

Jessie shook her head.

"I'd like you to magic us a treehouse to play in," said Ali.

"That's a good idea," said Jessie. "There's a big tree near my house. It could go there."

"I can't magic something out of nothing," Magicat moaned. "I need the right ingredients."

"Can you magic a treehouse out of this shed?" asked Jessie.

"That's a great idea," said Magicat.

"You'd better make sure Eddie Biggs doesn't see," Ali warned.

Jessie looked out of the shed window. There was no one in Eddie's garden and all the curtains in his house were drawn. "It's OK," she said. "They must have gone out."

Magicat stretched. Then he jumped up onto a stool, poked his tail out of the shed window and pointed it at the tree:

These children need a place to play,
Not a bed or stack of hay,
A magic cave in a tree,
Will be the perfect place to wee ...

40

"I think you mean *be* not *wee*," said Jessie. She and Ali giggled.

"It's not funny," said Magicat crossly.

He began again:

These children need a place to play,
Not a bed or stack of hay,
A magic cave in a tree,
Will be the perfect place to BE.

Magicat's fur stood on end. His green eyes shone bright. Sparks flew from his tail. There was a loud whooshing noise from under their feet.

BOOM!

"It sounds like a spaceship taking off," said Ali.

The shed shook, then rose slowly up into the air.

Jessie looked out of the window. "We're flying!"

The shed went up and up, past the bushes, higher than the fence and over to the big tree in Jessie's garden.

"Can we go to the moon?" said Ali.

"No. Not today," said Magicat.

For a minute, the shed floated in the air above a big branch that stretched towards Jessie's house, then it shook a bit and landed in the tree.

PLONK!

Ali stood up and went over to the shed window. "This is great. It's the best treehouse ever!"

"Well done, Magicat!" Jessie gave him a kiss on the nose.

"Yes, I have done well," said Magicat. He rubbed his paws together. "Now let's do some more magic. No one's going to bother us here."

Just then the door to the shed flew open.

"Gotcha!" said a voice.

It was Eddie Biggs!

CHAPTER 6

Magicat Escapes

"Meow," Magicat said. Just in time he'd remembered not to speak.

Eddie crawled into the shed.

Jessie noticed he was panting and he had twigs and leaves in his hair – he must have climbed up the tree.

"What are you doing here, Eddie?" Jessie gasped. "I thought you were out."

Eddie looked smug. "That's what I wanted you to think. I've been spying on you. I want to know what's going on."

"Nothing," Ali and Jessie said together.

"Rubbish," Eddie said. "I saw you collecting junk."

Phew! thought Jessie. Maybe Eddie hadn't seen the shed fly into the tree!

"What's wrong with collecting junk?" Ali asked.

Eddie gave a shrug. "I want to know what it's for," he said in a sly way.

Both Ali and Jessie were silent. Eddie mustn't know the junk was for Magicat's spells. Or that Magicat was, well, magic!

"And then I heard a big bang," said Eddie.

Jessie and Ali looked at one another. Things weren't turning out too well.

"That was me falling over," Ali said.

"Sure it was," said Eddie with a laugh. "And I'm a banana."

Magicat scratched his ear. He was thinking how much better Eddie would look as a banana than as a boy. Maybe he should turn him into one.

"Yeah, well, Eddie, that's all very interesting but we've got to go for lunch now," Jessie said.

Eddie didn't budge. "And *then* I saw the shed take off and fly into the tree." He folded his arms and gave a nasty grin. "How do you explain *that?*"

Jessie gulped. He *had* seen the shed fly after all! "It was windy," she said.

"*Very* windy," Ali agreed, nodding hard. "I think it might have been a hurricane."

"More like a tornado," Jessie said. "It lifted the whole shed up. Boom. Just like that."

"No, it didn't," Eddie said. "There wasn't any wind."

"Well, maybe not in *your* garden," Jessie said. "But there definitely was in ours."

Eddie ignored her. "I know what it really was." He pointed a finger at Magicat. "It was *him*."

Magicat froze. What should he do now?

"*HIM?!*" Jessie pretended to sound shocked. "What are you talking about? He's just a normal cat."

Normal cat, thought Magicat. *That's it. Act normal!* He began chasing a beetle round the floor.

"So why's he got a cauldron?" Eddie wanted to know.

"It's not *his* cauldron," Ali said. "We were playing witches and wizards. Just like on Halloween."

"Then how come there were sparks coming out of his tail?" said Eddie.

The two friends looked at each other for help. What could they say?

"It was one of Ali's tricks," said Jessie.

"I don't believe you," Eddie said. "Anyway, where did that cat actually come from?"

"I don't know," Jessie fibbed. "He just sort of arrived."

"Well, now he's just going to sort of leave," said Eddie. "With me." He made a grab for Magicat and caught him by the tail.

Magicat spun round. Now he *really* wanted to turn Eddie Biggs into a banana! Only he couldn't because he didn't know that spell and, even if he did, he knew he wasn't allowed to talk.

So he scratched Eddie instead.

"YEOW!" yelled Eddie, and let go of Magicat's tail.

"Serves you right!" Jessie shouted. "He's our cat. Leave him alone."

"No way!" Eddie made another grab for Magicat. The shed rocked.

"Be careful or it will all fall down," Ali shouted.

And spoil my magic cave, thought Magicat. *Forget that!*

He shot past Eddie and out of the shed door onto the branch.

Eddie chased after him.

Magicat raced along the branch towards Jessie's house.

Eddie crawled after him.

Up ahead, Magicat saw that the attic window was open. There was just enough space for a small cat to get through into the house. Magicat ran along the branch and squeezed in.

From inside the shed Jessie and Ali watched him. They really didn't want Eddie to get him.

"Eddie'll give up now," said Jessie when she saw Magicat's tail vanish into the house. "He'll never get through there. He's far too big."

"I'm not so sure about that," said Ali. "Look!"

Jessie gasped. Eddie had bust the attic window open. He climbed inside.

"Come on, Ali!" shouted Jessie. "Magicat needs help." Ali and Jessie made their way along the branch. They peered into the attic. The attic was full of cardboard boxes and bags of old toys. It was almost as full of junk as Ali's garden!

Eddie was chasing Magicat round and round. Magicat jumped from box to box so that Eddie couldn't grab his tail. Eddie puffed after him, kicking stuff out of the way with his big boots. His face was red from all the running he was having to do. He never normally did any exercise except chew gum.

"What shall we do?" Jessie whispered.

Eddie didn't look like he was planning to give up any time soon. And every time Magicat made for the window to escape, Eddie blocked his way.

"Don't worry. I've got a trick we can use."

Ali felt in his pockets and brought out a bag. He showed it to Jessie. Jessie grinned.

Marbles!

Ali threw the marbles into the attic. The tiny glass balls fell all over the wooden floor.

"AAARRRRRRGGGGGHHHHH!"

Eddie slipped on the marbles. His feet slid all over the place. Even his big boots couldn't stop him. He shot towards the window.

Ali and Jessie leaned back.

"AAARRRRRGGGGHHHHHHHHH!" Eddie flew out of the window and over the fence.

BOING!

He bounced off the trampoline.

SPLAT!

He landed on his bottom in the compost heap.

"Nice trick," Magicat said to Ali. He'd been watching with them from the window. "Now how about some real magic?"

"Like what?" said Ali.

Magicat's eyes gleamed. "How about I turn Eddie into a banana?"

CHAPTER 7
Magicat is Home Alone

A few days later, while Jessie was having breakfast, Magicat sat on the table next to her and stared at the fruit bowl on the kitchen table.

"I'm not going to turn Eddie into a banana," he said.

"Good," said Jessie as she slurped the cold milk from the bottom of her bowl of cereal. They had kept out of trouble so far. She wanted to keep it that way.

"I'll turn him into a pineapple instead."

"NO!" said Jessie. "You're not going to turn Eddie into anything. He'll know that you're definitely magic and he'll hate it if you make him look silly."

"He doesn't have to look in the mirror."

"But people will laugh at him. And then he'll do something awful to you."

"He won't be able to do very much because he'll be a pineapple," Magicat said.

"He won't be a pineapple because you're not going to turn him into a pineapple," said Jessie.

"Hmm," said Magicat, and he got on with cleaning his fur. Jessie took her cereal bowl and spoon and put them in the dishwasher.

"What if I just turn his head into a pineapple?" Magicat asked.

Jessie couldn't help laughing. But then she looked hard at Magicat.

"We don't want any more problems. Just keep away from Eddie, OK? I had enough trouble trying to explain to Mum and Dad how the shed ended up in the tree. It was lucky *they* believed me about the tornado."

Just then Dad came into the kitchen.

"Are you ready to go, Jessie?"

"Go where?" said Jessie.

Dad looked surprised.

"Into town. To buy some fireworks. It's bonfire night, remember?"

She did remember now. She and Ali had been having so much fun with Magicat that she had forgotten it was bonfire night and Dad had promised to buy fireworks. Most of the time Jessie loved to go shopping but today she wanted to stay with Magicat.

"I don't want to go shopping," she said to Dad.

Dad looked even more surprised.

"That's not like you, Jessie. I thought you liked shopping, especially for fireworks."

"I do, but I want to be with Magicat. Can't we take him shopping?"

"Meow," Magicat begged. It was so annoying, pretending he couldn't talk.

"NO!" said Dad. "Have you ever seen a cat in the shops?"

"Meow, meow," Magicat yowled. Of course cats went to shops, at least they did in Magic Land.

"I've only seen a toy one," Jessie admitted.

No cats in shops! thought Magicat. *How silly.*

"Well, if you don't want to buy fireworks, I'll go and see if there are any left over from last year in the attic."

"NO!" shouted Jessie. If Dad went into the attic, he'd see the broken window. "I've changed my mind. I will come shopping."

Dad frowned. "You're in a funny mood this morning, Jessie," he said.

"I'm just excited to have Magicat here," said Jessie, and she stroked Magicat's ears.

"He'll still be here when you get back," said Dad.

"Yes, he WILL," said Jessie, and looked straight at Magicat.

Magicat knew what that look meant. It meant: *you will stay here and not go out and not do any magic and not have anything to do with Eddie Biggs.* He jumped off the table and walked off in a huff with his tail in the air.

Jessie and Dad left a few minutes later. Magicat settled down on the sofa. He thought he might watch TV. He was trying to work out how to turn it on when the window opened and a letter flew in.

He jumped down off the sofa and went to have a look. It was addressed to him in big letters: MAGICAT. Magicat's heart started to beat faster. It must be from Wenna Witch! He slit it open with his claw. Magicat read the letter as fast as he could:

Hello Magicat,

I'm glad to hear you're safe. I'm coming to get you soon. Look out for me – I'll be dressed as a human. Don't get behind with your studies! Work hard and remember to practise every day!

Wenna Witch

Magicat turned the paper over. On the back was the spell Wenna Witch wanted him to practise. He read it to himself:

Find a top, if not a skirt,
Then a mug, not full of dirt.
Wrap the mug up in the clothes,
Then sing a tune or song you know.

Give your tail a little shake,

Something different you will make.

The spell sounded exciting! Magicat forgot
that Jessie didn't want him to do any spells.
He raced upstairs to Jessie's room. There was
a mug by the bed and one of Jessie's T-shirts on
the floor. He wrapped the mug in the T-shirt
and started to meow his favourite tune:

Twinkle, Twinkle, little star

What a magic cat you are

Up above the world you fly

On a broomstick, my oh my

Twinkle, Twinkle, little star

What a magic cat you are.

Magicat gave his tail a little shake, like it said
in the spell. His fur stood on end. His green
eyes shone bright.

Suddenly he heard a noise behind him.

THUMP! THUMP! THUMP!

Magicat turned round. Eddie Biggs was marching across the bedroom towards him in his big boots. He must have got in through the attic window again and come down the stairs!

"Hello, cat," said Eddie. He was chewing gum.

Eddie put his hands out. Magicat felt really scared. He pointed his tail at Eddie. Sparks flew from the end. All of a sudden there was a flash.

FLASH!

And a bang.

BANG!

The room was silent, apart from a little scuttling noise. Magicat looked down.

There was a spider just in front of his paw.

The spider was chewing some gum.

It was a spider called Eddie.

CHAPTER 8

Tacijam!

When Jessie got back from her shopping trip, Magicat was lying on the comfy cushion in her bedroom, fast asleep. His front paw was out in front of him as if something was trapped underneath it. Magicat opened one eye.

"I've got a surprise for you," he said.

Magicat lifted his paw and out from under it scuttled an enormous hairy spider. It had a mean look about it. Beside it was an old piece of gum.

"Wow! Where did you catch that?" Jessie asked.

"Well, I didn't exactly catch it," Magicat admitted. "It sort of caught me. Or at least it tried to."

"What do you mean?" Jessie said.

Magicat let out a heavy sigh. Jessie was going to be cross. "It wasn't my fault," he said. "I didn't *mean* to turn Eddie into a spider."

"That's Eddie Biggs?" Jessie gasped.

Magicat nodded. "He crept up on me while I was practising my magic."

"I told you not to do any magic when I was out." Jessie frowned.

"I know you did, and I wasn't going to," Magicat replied. "But my witch sent me a letter and told me to practise my spells. I got the letter when you were out."

Jessie folded her arms. "You have to turn Eddie back into a boy," she said.

"Can't we just let him go in the garden?" Magicat said in a very small voice.

"No, we can't."

"Oh, all right," Magicat agreed. "But I'll have to do it in the shed. I need somewhere witchy."

"What ingredients do you need for the spell?" Jessie asked.

"A mug and one of your T-shirts."

"Is that all?"

"Yes."

Jessie put the spider, the chewing gum, the mug and the T-shirt in her rucksack and took them downstairs.

Magicat padded after her, the letter in his mouth. They went out of the back door into the garden.

Ali was just coming through the fence from his dad's junk yard. He was carrying a rope ladder. "I found this," he said. "I thought it might be useful."

"Very useful," Jessie said. "We need to get up to the shed as fast as we can." She told Ali what had happened while she was out.

Ali whistled. "A spider!" he said. Then he laughed. "I thought you were going to turn Eddie into a banana, Magicat!"

"I was, only Jessie wouldn't let me," Magicat said. "She wouldn't even let me turn him into a pineapple." He looked hard at Jessie. "Actually, if you think about it, all this is really *your* fault. This would never have happened if Eddie was a bit of fruit."

Jessie sighed. Magicat always liked to have the last word about everything!

Ali climbed up the tree and fixed the rope ladder to a big branch. Magicat followed him. Jessie climbed up the ladder and they all went into the shed. They closed the door.

"Put Eddie in the cauldron so he can't escape," Magicat ordered.

Jessie plopped the spider into the cauldron. It ran to and fro but it couldn't get up the slippery sides.

"Now wrap the mug in the T-shirt."

Ali put them in the cauldron beside the spider.

"Stand back," Magicat warned.

Jessie and Ali moved far away from the cauldron.

"Cover your eyes," Magicat said. He sang his tune:

Twinkle, Twinkle, little star
What a magic cat you are
Up above the world you fly
On a broomstick, my oh my
Twinkle, Twinkle, little star
What a magic cat you are.

"Those aren't the right words," said Jessie.

"They are when I sing them," Magicat retorted. "Don't interrupt."

Magicat's fur stood on end. His green eyes shone bright. He sang his tune and shook his tail.

There was a flash.

FLASH!

And a bang.

BANG!

"Did it work?" Ali asked.

"Not really," Magicat said as he peeped over the edge of the cauldron.

The children came forward and peered in. They gasped. Now Eddie was a frog!

"I'll try again," said Magicat. "Don't interrupt me this time."

The children stood back.

FLASH!!

BANG!!

"Oh dear," said Magicat.

This time Eddie was an enormous beetle!

"Maybe if you want to turn him *back* into a boy, you need to do the *spell* backwards?" Jessie said.

"That's a good idea," Magicat agreed. "Which bits, though?"

The children looked at the letter and Ali read:

Find a top, if not a skirt,
Then a mug, not full of dirt.
Wrap the mug up in the clothes,
Then sing a tune or song you know.
Give your tail a little shake,
Something different you will make.

"But I can't wrap the mug round the T-shirt," Magicat said, puzzled.

The children looked at the letter.

"I know!" Ali exclaimed. "Top spelled backwards is pot!"

"And mug spelled backwards is gum!" Jessie cried. "That's what you need to turn Eddie back into a boy, Magicat! Instead of a top and a mug, you have to use a pot and a piece of gum!"

"I knew that," Magicat said. "I was just testing you."

Jessie and Ali gave each other a look. Magicat didn't like to admit he was wrong about anything!

"Eddie had gum," Magicat said. "He was chewing it when he got in the way."

"I've got it!" Jessie pulled the gum out of her rucksack.

"And here's a plant pot!" said Ali.

Jessie put the gum and the pot in the cauldron with the beetle. Ali took out the mug and the T-shirt.

Magicat got ready to do the spell.

"Hang on a minute," Ali said. "Can we add something to make Eddie a bit nicer?"

"We could try putting something sweet in the cauldron," said Magicat.

"Good idea," Jessie said.

Ali put his hand into his pocket. There was a sweet they had been given on Halloween! He threw it into the cauldron with the other ingredients.

The two children stood back.

Magicat sang his tune.

FLASH!!

BANG!!

This time it did work. Eddie Biggs exploded from the cauldron.

Ali and Jessie leaned back to let him pass.

"AAARRRRRGGGGHHHHHHHHHH!" Eddie flew out of the shed door and over the fence.

BOING!

He bounced off the trampoline.

SPLAT!

He landed on his bottom in the compost heap.

The children roared with laughter.

"Now that," said Magicat, sounding very pleased with himself, "is what I call a spell."

CHAPTER 9

Magicat the Magic Cat

"That was brilliant," said Jessie happily.

"It was *really* brilliant," said Magicat. "You see, I'm very good at spells once I know what to do."

"I wish you knew a spell for fixing attic windows," Ali said.

Magicat jumped back onto his feet.

"I do!" said Magicat. "Now I know that you can undo what's happened if you say your spell backwards, I can fix anything. Watch!"

Magicat pointed his tail at the window and said: "Wodniw eht xif!!!"

Magicat's fur stood on end. His green eyes shone bright. Sparks flew from his tail.

FLASH!

BANG!

"There," said Magicat. "One fixed window."

The children stared at the window and smiled. It looked perfect.

"How did you do that spell?" asked Ali. "It sounded like you were talking rubbish."

"It isn't rubbish if you say it the other way round," Magicat said.

"Wodniw eht xif," said Jessie to herself. And then her face broke into a big smile. "Fix the window. You said 'Fix the window' backwards!"

She went over to Magicat and gave him a big hug. "I'm so happy you fell into Ali's treat bucket."

"So am I," said Magicat. He rolled over so Jessie could stroke his tummy.

Ali came and joined in. "Me too!"

"You've made our lives so much more exciting," said Jessie.

"And more fun," said Ali.

"Hell-o-o," someone called out from below.

"Is that Eddie?" whispered Jessie. "He sounds so nice!"

Ali gave a shrug. "Maybe adding the sweet to the spell worked! Let's go and see."

"OK, but be careful, Magicat," Jessie warned. "Don't talk in front of him. And no more spells."

"All right," Magicat agreed.

Eddie Biggs was waiting for them at the bottom of the tree.

He held out his hand to stroke Magicat. "Hello, lovely little cat!" said Eddie.

"Don't hurt him," Jessie told Eddie. She didn't quite believe what she was seeing. Eddie seemed to have turned into a nice boy.

"Of course I won't hurt him," said Eddie. "Why would I hurt a lovely little cat like him?"

Eddie stroked Magicat. Magicat didn't purr because he still didn't like Eddie very much even if Eddie liked him.

Jessie was amazed.

"Would you like to come and play in my garden?" Eddie said to Jessie. "I've got a swing and a trampoline. Ali and the cat can come too, of course."

Jessie had never been into Eddie's garden and she had always been scared of Eddie. But now he seemed so different and she'd always wanted a go on his trampoline.

"I'll ask my dad," she said.

"And I'll ask my mum," said Ali.

"I'll look after the cat," said Eddie with a lovely smile.

Magicat glared at Eddie. He hadn't forgotten how he'd chased him and grabbed his tail. He hoped Jessie and Ali would be back soon. One sweet on a horrible boy like Eddie wasn't going to last long but he couldn't say that to Jessie and Ali because he wasn't allowed to talk in front of other people!

Jessie and Ali went to ask their parents. Magicat was alone with Eddie. Eddie was still smiling at him sweetly.

"Don't be scared."

Eddie held out his hand and very gently stroked Magicat's head.

Magicat purred. Maybe Eddie really was nice after all.

Suddenly Eddie's smile vanished. He popped another piece of chewing gum in his mouth.

Uh oh, thought Magicat. *I knew it.*

The sweet was wearing off.

Sure enough, Eddie grabbed at Magicat's tail. Magicat jumped away just in time.

"Come here, cat!" Eddie shouted.

Magicat shot off across the lawn.

"What are you doing?" shouted Jessie as she ran back out of the house. "Leave him alone!"

"Why should I?" said Eddie. The mean look was back on his face.

"Because you're sweet now," said Ali as he came through the fence from his house.

"Who says? I'm not sweet," said Eddie.

"You soon will be," said a loud voice.

The children turned round. There was a lollipop lady standing in the garden! How had she got there? She hadn't been there a few minutes ago! And she wasn't holding a round metal sign – instead she held a giant yellow lollipop. She pointed it towards Eddie. Her eyes turned green. Her hair stood on end.

FLASH!

BANG!

The lollipop fizzed like a firework. Bits of sugar rained down on Eddie's head. He smiled sweetly.

"That should do it," said the woman.

"Thanks, Wenna!" said Magicat. He rushed over to the lollipop lady and rubbed himself against her legs. "You came just in time!"

Jessie and Ali gasped. The lollipop lady must be Wenna Witch! They looked at one another. *But that meant ...*

"Do you really have to go, Magicat?" Jessie said sadly.

"Of course I do," said Magicat. "I've got to go to school like you and learn how to spell."

"But when will you be back?" said Ali.

"Next Halloween," said Magicat. He pointed his tail at Eddie. "And if he's naughty again next year, I really will turn him into a banana."

They all heard a bang in the sky and looked up. It was almost dark but the sky was full of bright colours.

"Time to go," said Wenna, "the fireworks are starting. Everyone will be too busy looking at them to notice us flying back to Magic Land."

Jessie and Ali gave Magicat a kiss on the nose. "See you next year," they said. "Don't forget to write."

Wenna sat on the lollipop stick. Magicat jumped on behind. The lollipop began to fizz.

VRROOOOOMMMMMMMM!

Wenna and Magicat flew off over the trees and into the night sky.

Eddie came over. "Don't be sad," he said to Jessie. "I'm sure he'll be back."

Just then Mum and Dad came out of the house with a box of fireworks.

"It's nice to see you three getting along,"
said Mum. "Would you like to stay and watch
the fireworks with us, Eddie?"

"Yes, please," said Eddie.

Jessie felt very sad that Magicat had gone but she smiled. At least Eddie wasn't a bully any more.

Dad was looking up at the sky. "Look at the stars," he said. "I've never seen that before. They're in the shape of a big banana."

The children looked up. They didn't tell Dad but what he was looking at wasn't the stars. It was sparks of magic.

"It's Magicat," Jessie whispered. "He's saying goodbye."

Our books are tested
for children and young people by
children and young people.

Thanks to everyone who consulted on
a manuscript for their time and effort in
helping us to make our books better
for our readers.